Heart of the Storm

a Night Stalker story
by
M. L. Buchman

Buchman Bookworks

Other works by M.L. Buchman

The Night Stalkers
The Night Is Mine
I Own the Dawn
Daniel's Christmas
Wait Until Dark
Frank's Independence Day
Peter's Christmas
Take Over at Midnight
Light Up the Night

Firehawks
Pure Heat
Wildfire at Dawn
Full Blaze

Angelo's Hearth
Where Dreams are Born
Where Dreams Reside
Maria's Christmas Table
Where Dreams Unfold
Where Dreams Are Written

Dieties Anonymous
Cookbook from Hell: Reheated
Saviors 101

Thrillers
Swap Out!

One Chef!
Two Chef!

SF/F Titles
Nara
Monk's Maze

Five Years Ago

1

Major Michael Gibson of U.S. Army's Delta Force was at eleven thousand feet, less than two hundred feet below the summit of Little Tahoma Peak when he heard the distress call on his radio. It was pure chance that he heard anything.

The January winds were howling down upon him, caught in the funnel of Little Tahoma and Mount Rainier's nearby peak that climbed another three thousand feet above him. The Arctic northerly, driving in the frigid Canadian air and dumping several feet of overnight snow, still howled beneath a sky so blue it could have been a child's spilled paints.

At least it was blue where last night's storm scrubbed the sky clean before departing southward to rush over Mount St. Helens and Mount Hood on its way to bury the Siskiyou Mountains of northern California. The northern sky already looked to be gearing up for the next onslaught through the Cascade Mountain Range.

Michael had escaped the ceaseless roar of the icy wind when he tucked down behind a sharp crag for a minute to chew on an energy bar and drink some water. He wasn't hungry, or thirsty. But his high-altitude survival training had reinforced what he'd already known—by the time you noticed hunger or thirst at altitude, it was already too late. And this broken bit of volcanic rock was probably his last refuge before the summit—two hundred feet and perhaps an hour and a half above him. He should have just enough time to take the peak and get clear. Maybe he could cut the ascent time down to an hour.

Hunkered down behind his rock, he was offered one of the best views on the planet. From southeast sweeping around to southwest, the lush forests of Washington State spread over the rugged terrain. Doug Fir, Larch, White Pine, all underlaid with Oregon grape and blackberries so thick that even a Special Operations soldier would go looking for a way around.

North down to northwest revealed relative flatlands, no less green. In the far distance the waters of Puget Sound glittered beneath the low morning sun. If he'd been willing to remove his snow goggles and pull out his binoculars, Tacoma and Seattle would come easily into view despite the fifty miles of distance. As it was, the big airplanes climbing out of SeaTac Airport were the only encroachment from the big cities; he could feel the passengers snapping blurred pictures through plastic windows from their warm, plush seats as they flew over.

Immediately below him in all directions were the glaciers of Mt. Rainier National Park. From his vantage point high on Little Tahoma's flank, Emmons, Ingraham, Cowlitz, and the bound shoulder of

Nisqually Glacier lay like a broken carpet of blinding white; constantly tearing at the volcano's rocky sides to bring the old girl down. *Good luck with that.*

Straight ahead Mount Rainier rose to fourteen thousand-four hundred feet, her rounded peak in stark relief—permanently-glaciered blinding white against the blue sky. He'd ridden out last night's brief but vicious blow at the base of Little Tahoma in a snow cave.

He found a small patch of snow to sit on among the high rock to give his legs a moment or two to recover while he ate.

His goal was to hit Little Tahoma Peak today, and then get off the mountain. He'd originally thought to climb Rainier as well while he was up here, but he could see the northern horizon already graying up even more in the five minutes he'd crouched here. Tonight's storm was predicted to make last night's look like a mere flurry. It would lock out the mountain to even the most ambitious climbers for days. And he was due back in the Congo Rainforest hunting genocidal warlords soon.

Michael listened for a response to the radio distress call. He should have heard it if there was one. From his perch he had sweeping coverage of the entire west of the Rainier down to Camp Muir at ten thousand feet and Paradise at five thousand.

The call repeated.

Silence, except for the wind raging to either side of his boulder. The park rangers clearly hadn't heard it though the call had been on the frequency that everyone on the mountain was required to monitor.

Everyone on the mountain.

It was the first day of the New Year, there were only five people listed in the Park Office's register. An elderly couple in their fifties hiking to Camp Muir for an overnight. A young couple, Charlene and Fred Moore with a climbing pass for the summit. And him.

Reluctantly, sorry to break away from the peace of his solo climb, he pulled out his radio and fitted the earpiece; partly because it used less power than the speaker, and partly his military training to not give away his position was so deeply ingrained—despite being on friendly soil.

"To distress call on Rainier. This is Michael, go ahead."

"Oh thank god!" A woman's voice crackled over the earbud. "Fred has fallen into a crevasse and I can't get him out. He's trapped and hurt. His radio must be broken, but we can sort of shout in between the wind gusts. At least I think so. It's hard to tell. Please, come. Please. We need help."

Michael listened for a moment. The wind wasn't gusting much. More of a steady howl.

"Okay, I need you to remain calm," he thought back to the register at the park office, "Charlene. We're going to go through this by the numbers. First, are you personally safe? Solidly anchored and warm enough?"

"Yes, we're both snapped into an ice screw. I managed to get a piton into the rock and have a backup line anchored there. And its Charli."

"Good," more together than he'd expected. "Now, where are you?"

She wasn't sure. The trip had been Fred's idea, no surprise there. In Michael's experience women were generally too sensible to do something like climb Rainier in the dead of winter. Though they weren't sensible enough not to follow along when a likely male beckoned them into doing something stupid.

For himself, he'd wanted to keep his snow and ice skills up. He could feel them melting away under ops conducted in the heat and humidity of the Congolese rainforest, so he'd gone for a winter tromp up Rainier.

But if she'd known to anchor herself more securely before calling for help, she wasn't a helpless soul traveling on her husband's whim either.

So, they began playing the "what can you see" game in a world of ice, rock, and sky.

2

Captain Mark Henderson stood outside hangar 4-C and stared up at the northern sky. He debated whether to call for a training sortie or to give his crew the night off.

It was midday and he was supposed to be sleeping, just as they were now, but upper brass never did understand SOAR. They'd rousted him with a question that could have been asked and answered by e-mail anytime in the next week if some Colonel hadn't had a hair up his ass.

The U.S. Army 160th Special Aviation Regiment specialized in one thing, nighttime helicopter operations. They did it better than anyone on the planet. That's how they earned the Night Stalkers nickname. They'd flown into hundreds of places that they could never admit to, delivering Delta, SEAL, and other U.S. Special Operations assets to places no one else could get them into...or back out of alive.

But that meant he was supposed to be asleep right now like the rest of his crew. Not that he'd been sleeping much lately. Three months ago, the powers that be had decided that SOAR needed a fifth battalion. It was to be based in Tacoma, Washington at Joint Base Lewis-McChord. The 5th was to have four companies and he'd gotten the tap to lead "D" Company.

His goal was simple. If SOAR were the best helicopter pilots on the planet, the 5th Battalion's D Company was going to be the best in SOAR.

Period.

There would be no need to brag.

They'd earn it.

He had argued for and, surprisingly considering the layers of brass involved, been given the go-ahead to assemble a mixed company—the only one in the entire regiment. Most of SOAR was structured with one type of helicopter per company. Hell, the entire 2nd Battalion only flew the massive twin-rotor Chinooks. If they needed a Black Hawk or a Little Bird, they had to go outside not just the company, but the battalion to borrow assets.

It made sense to the paper pushers. This way the 2nd Battalion only needed one set of spare parts, one set of mechanics.

Mark didn't give one damn about logistics.

Well, he did, but he cared far more about his ability to respond. Because the 5D was a unique experiment, they'd decided to cripple his ass by giving him fewer assets. They'd learn and change their tune soon enough. In the meantime, he was collecting the best of the best personnel he could find, anywhere. He called and they came running, whether or not he'd flown with them before. It was deeply gratifying because these guys really were good.

At the moment he had two Little Bird helicopters good for fast attacks and tight in-and-out tight scenarios, one of the big

Chinook heavy lifters, two transport Black Hawks, and his baby.

He needed to name her, but she was so perfect that he hadn't found the right name yet. She was one of the rarest helicopters on the planet. There were only a dozen of them and they were custom designed by SOAR for their exclusive usage. The Direct Action Penetrator DAP Hawk might look like a weaponized Sikorsky Black Hawk, but she wasn't even close. She was the most sophisticated, bad-ass helo ever launched into the night sky. And she was all his.

A lot of SOAR's company commanders led from the safety of a behind-the-lines observer seat. Mark planned to lead the 5D from the right-hand pilot's seat of the…

Damn! He really needed to name her.

He wouldn't mind a bad-ass nickname himself. He'd never picked one up along the way. Guys tried them on him, but they always faded away and he always drifted back to being Mark.

Wouldn't it be funny if he and his Hawk had the same cool name? That would really screw with people's minds.

He focused back on the graying sky to the north and pulled the leather bomber jacket his mother had given him for Christmas more tightly closed against the chill air. Puget Sound didn't hit freezing very often, even in mid-winter, but the day was struggling for twenty degrees this afternoon courtesy of a chill Canadian system sweeping down the Fraser River Valley.

He turned his head and spoke back over his shoulder to the DAP Hawk helicopter tucked away in hangar 4-C, "We fly tonight, girl."

The helo seemed to sleep more soundly for knowing that.

Yeah. SOAR was known for being able to go anywhere at any time. The U.S. Postal Service motto of rain, snow, sleet, etc. had nothing on what the 160th SOAR could do.

And very soon now, the 160th SOAR wouldn't have anyone able to match what Henderson's 5th Battalion D Company Night Stalkers could deliver.

3

Charli had calmed down the rest of the way when she realized that she could see Michael's position high on Little Tahoma Peak. That still hadn't given him much information on where she was.

They did finally narrow it down though.

Partly, the westering sun had revealed the snake-track shadow that their hike up had left through last night's thick powder, and partly Charli had kept her head.

"Disappointment Cleaver," she agreed when he mentioned that landmark. "Yes, my brother talked about that."

Not Mister and Missus.

"He said we were nearing the jump off point for the peak."

Top of the Cleaver, which put them past twelve thousand feet. The low-point saddle between his eleven thousand foot position and hers past twelve was down at ten thousand feet. An easy hour stroll down and back up if it wasn't all up in the rarefied atmosphere above ten thousand feet and the ice-bearing winds weren't howling like a demon across the face of fifty-degree slopes.

With his binoculars he finally pinned down their position, a dot of bright red parka against white snow. Just a mile away, as the raven flies.

He watched the snow spume outward in white-out clouds beneath the near hurricane force winds. Mt. Rainier stuck up past half-way to the jet stream and it wreaked havoc up here near the peak. Not even a raven could fly a straight line in this weather.

"Okay, I'm going to listen all the time, Charli. So if you have a problem, you can call me. But I want you to shut off your radio to save the battery," he had three spares with him, but Charli's were in the crevasse with her brother. "Each hour on the hour, you can check in with me. But I want you to have plenty of power for when I get close. Can you do that?"

She hadn't sounded happy, but she'd agreed and signed off.

He needed her to save her battery, but he also needed the silence. He had a long, technically tricky traverse down the slopes of Little Tahoma, then much higher up on Rainier's flank. It required concentration to plan and execute. Being in the quiet of the world was what he needed to—

"This is Mt. Rainier Rescue to Michael, come back."

So much for peace up on the mountain. It simply wasn't going to be that sort of day.

"Michael here."

"We couldn't hear the other half of the conversation. Please relay information and do not attempt solo rescue. We already have climbing rangers enroute."

He relayed the information about Charli's location and her brother's unknown condition. Then he waited through the long pause of silence. He knew what was coming and wanted to get moving, but once he did the wind would deafen him and he'd need both hands and his full attention on what he was doing. He was free-climbing solo. He hadn't brought great chunks of rope or enough gear so that he could rappel down from Little Tahoma and then abandon the gear to climb up Rainier.

"Uh, Roger that," the rangers finally responded. They might be good guys, but they were just Parkies and this was getting uglier by the moment.

Michael gave them another thirty seconds. *Enough.*

"Please transmit location and number of rescue climbers."

"We have two rescue-qualified climbing rangers leaving Longmire now."

Michael didn't need three minutes of silence to assess the situation. Current road conditions made that an hour drive to Paradise, then a three to five hour hike to Camp Muir. And that would place them five to six hours below Charli and Fred Moore's location. The storm was two hours out—

three if he was lucky, but it wasn't that kind of day.

"Helicopter support?"

"Not in these winds. They'll have to…"

Ride it out, the operator didn't need to say. One of them down in a crevasse and injured; the other exposed to the elements with night falling. It was their death warrant.

"Roger that," Michael considered for a moment. "Get your two park rangers to re-cover the couple who went up to Camp Muir. Do not send them up the mountain. I don't want to have to rescue four people. Out."

He tucked away his radio, the wrapper of his energy bar, and sipped some more water. Then he dug out a balaclava that covered everything except his snow goggles, and tugged on his gloves.

He had to keep the radio on in case Charli called.

The park rangers stop talking to him by the time he'd descended the first five hundred feet.

After that, he moved in peace.

Nothing but himself, the rock and ice, and the roar of Mother Nature as she veered the storm to drive straight onto the face of the mountain.

4

"You are a complete bastard making us fly in this shit." The new guy Tim Maloney came up to Mark as he waited by the DAP Hawk in the dark of the glowering afternoon sky.

It was blowing twenty, gusting thirty down here on the field.

Tim tapped a couple fingers to the brow of his helmet in a casual salute, "Damn but I like that in a commander."

Sergeants Crazy Tim Maloney and Big John Wallace had requested to come aboard as a package deal to fill the two crew-chief spots. He'd wanted Big John who had a reputation for being an ace mechanic. And after he'd seen how Tim handled a mini-gun—crazy or not he was damned good—decided to give them both a try.

Mark's co-pilot, a Lieutenant Richardson, also was shaking down well. He flew silent which Mark appreciated and was a steady hand on the cyclic in a tight spot.

It had only been a month but the team was mission ready by any standard he could come up with. There were still a lot of rough edges to polish off, but they were all of the sort that were only going to happen in combat.

Lots of combat.

Of course with multiple wars on top of the usual list of black ops, that polish would come all too soon.

Henderson managed not to laugh at Tim's comment, staying cool behind his mirrored Ray Bans as the afternoon light was shifting to evening. That's what a commander did. He wasn't one of the guys, he was the steady rock. He made sure he was always the best man on his team to give them something to trust and to strive for.

Under the heavy storm clouds, it was already growing dark.

"If you're too chicken to fly in this shit," he informed Tim doing his best not to smile, "you just let me know and I'll sign your ticket back to the 10th Mountain."

"Dude," Big John rolled up from completing the preflight inspection on the DAP Hawk to glare down at his buddy.

John stood at least six-four and was massively strong. It was a surprise every single time he managed to fit into the crew chief's seat close behind Henderson's piloting position.

Tim was equally broad-shouldered but at five-eight looked tiny next to his friend.

"You get us booted," John's voice was a low rumble, "and I am gonna sit on your head until all the stupid runs out your ass."

"I—"

"Let's saddle up," Mark cut Tim off granting the round to Big John. He'd long since learned that if he didn't choose a winner, these guys could go at it all night without missing a beat.

Once they were all in position and the intercom was up, he filled them in. "This is a test of the new systems you guys laid in. I want to be able to fly within three meters of plan in zero visibility. Fog, snow, I don't give a shit. I want to prove we can do it until we know it in our bones."

"Yes sir, Boss."

"She'll do it," John was very protective of his helo, just what you wanted in a chief mechanic.

Richardson kept his usual silence.

Mark cleared with the tower and lifted the DAP Hawk into thirty knots of nasty. The rain was trying to decide if it was sleet, and the gusts were working to tie the clouds into intricate Christmas bows. Perfect weather for a test flight.

They'd start in the waning daylight and work the skills right into darkness. By sunrise they'd have it down.

They'd own it.

Without his needing to ask, Richardson had the terrain-following radar active and had layered it on the terrain map programmed into the computer.

Mark started at fifty feet above the pines and laid down the hammer, turning southeast to get some terrain-following practice in the foothills of the Cascade Range.

5

Michael was down off Little Tahoma Peak in forty minutes.

The blue was gone from the sky. He couldn't tell if there was new snow falling from the clouds yet. Maybe it was just that he'd descended from the rocky buttress of Little Tahoma down onto the Emmons Glacier and it was last night's snowfall blowing sideways.

After he clipped on his crampons, he spent twenty precious minutes finding his way through the serac field. The massive blocks of ice thrown up by the glacier impacting the uphill slopes of Little Tahoma had created a near impenetrable field of house-sized chunks all looking to spill downslope at the slightest provocation.

It was a risky route. He'd calculated that against the additional time required to descend another thousand feet to where the Ingraham Glacier trailed placidly along Little Tahoma's lower reaches, cross safely, and only then start the much longer climb up to Disappointment Cleaver. He knew Charli Moore wasn't in a position to wait that long.

Also, the lengthier and safer descent would place the bastion of rock between them and block radio contact. The last thing he needed was for her to panic.

At precisely one hour she called in, just as he cleared the serac field.

"I'm hoping to be there before your next check-in call," he assured her and then calculated the chances of delivering on that and didn't like them.

A mile away up a forty-five degree slope. Climb the stairs of the Empire State Building five times. Except the stairs were steeper than normal ones built by humans, made of ice, and filled with hidden crevasses crossed by precarious snow bridges.

Michael checked his map for his current position and took a careful compass reading. Then he set the GPS as a backup.

By the next check-in, if he wasn't there, he'd be able to tell her how soon in minutes.

He unfolded the long aluminum pole and snapped it together so that he could test the snow before he stepped on it. Taking his ice axe firmly in his other hand, he set out at a fast clip.

It would be best if he crossed as much territory as he could before the storm hit. The gray clouds were already flattening the light, making it hard to see just how high to raise a foot to make the next step.

Sometimes the sun broke through the ragged southern edges of the clouds, but it soon disappeared behind the high shoulder of the mountain and he was on his own.

That was one of the things that had drawn him to join Delta Force. Unlike the SEALs who trained in groups of four, six, and twelve as their ultimate team, Delta was trained to survive and complete the mission at all costs—even when it was just one man.

Michael had always enjoyed the structure of the Army, but the "group think" had never fit him well. Delta, who called themselves simply The Unit, had answered much of that need within him. He trained with the very best and could slide seamlessly into any size team when required. But his favorite mode was to walk alone into the heart of a hostile city, see what had to be seen, perhaps kill who needed to be killed, and walk back out with no one the wiser.

Counter-terrorism.

The terrorists followed no set rules. Battlefield tactics didn't apply. The Unit of Delta Force had been built from the ground up by its own soldiers with that in mind. When—

He hesitated.

Froze in place.

Then took a careful step backward.

His testing pole had gone too deeply into the snow ahead of him. He eased back another step and whacked the pole like a whipping cane flat against the snow ahead of him a half dozen times. The long sideways span of the slope silently disappeared from in front of him. The exposed crevasse was only a yard wide, but it would have swallowed him happily.

He could traverse sideways looking for a crossing, which could lead him far astray from his intended path. And chew up valuable time that Charli Moore didn't have.

Instead he took a moment to pack the snow on his side of the crevasse and double-checked his grip on his ice axe. He used the packed snow as a sprinter's lane, kicked hard off the rim of the gap in the glacier, and landed cleanly on two feet on the high side.

He lunged upward onto his stomach to spread his weight and buried his ice axe as far upslope as he could.

The snow held. He crawled a dozen paces further upslope before returning to his feet. He stood in place a moment and checked his crampons. The straps were tight and the closures were frozen in place, which fine. He rubbed the tip of his nose through the thick balaclava for a moment to warm it up, then continued upward.

Michael had joined the Army straight out of college at eighteen. And gone Delta as soon as they let him, at twenty-three. After five years…

It wasn't going stale.

Not exactly.

The ops were too challenging for that. The variety too interesting. But there was a sameness to it. The Unit had some of the very best soldiers on the planet and he was pretty much the top of that heap.

That wasn't ego.

He reached a broad crevasse crossed by a narrow snow bridge; snow that had packed into the perfect pattern to hold shape over the gap. But would it stay there? A couple jabs with his pole were encouraging.

His commanders said he was the best—consistently.

He ran an ice screw into the low side of the crevasse, tied a line to it, and made a midpoint loop to attach to his harness. He crossed carefully and made it. So he ran in another ice screw well above the crevasse and tied the far end of his line to that. He then crossed once more to the low side of the bridge to recover the first ice screw, he had few to spare.

His fellow operators always looked to him to take the lead.

The bridge gave out on the third crossing, but he fell only a few feet before the line snapped taut. He hauled himself to the upper ice screw, recovered it, and moved ahead upslope. The fall barely registered. Little things like that didn't when he was in the zone. You got through the mission by doing what had to be done. *Whatever* had to be done.

It was fine for everyone else when you were at the head of the pack. But who was going to push him to be better? There was only so much you could do to drive your own self ahead.

He circled a serac as big as C-130 cargo plane that was tipped so far forward it could well roll down the slope in the next gust. It was eerily quiet crossing underneath its looming mass.

The fresh blast of needle-sharp ice crystals as he stepped from behind it only served to remind him that the storm's hammer had hit the mountain now, with a vengeance.

He double-checked his compass, considered how far the serac had been from the rocky outcropping of Disappointment Cleaver and knew he was off pace. He would not be up to where Charli and Fred's lives hung in the balance before the next radio check in.

But he'd be close.

So would the darkness.

6

Mark Henderson hovered three feet above the empty football field at Enumclaw High School. They had made it flying totally blind, at least he had been blind. Richardson had kept a lookout just in case.

But Mark had slid down the outer sun shield on his helmet's visor and concentrated on the FLIR terrain data projected on the inside of his helmet, pretending it was pitch dark rather than a stormy evening.

Per SOAR standards, he'd arrived within thirty seconds of the arbitrarily set time… barely. He'd have to work on that. That was one of the promises the Night Stalkers of SOAR made to their Special Operations customers, to always be there within thirty seconds of schedule…no matter where "there" was. No matter what the weather or the enemy were doing. "Landing zone is too hot" simply wasn't in the Night Stalkers' vocabulary.

"Okay. Set me three geographic points. Who knows this area?"

"There's this crazy bike ride out here that a friend was telling me about," Tim spoke up over the intercom. "It's called the Rimrock or the…no, the RAMROD. It stands for Ride Around Mt. Rainier in One Day."

"Bike ride?" John cut in. "Hell, Tim. If your bike is so slow it can't do that, you need to upgrade your scooter."

"Not motorcycle, dude. Bicycle. It's like two hundred miles and tons of vertical climb. One hellacious lap of the mountain."

"I like it," Mark decided. "Give me three target points."

Richardson was working the maps. "Top of Cayuse Pass." He marked it on the display. Mark kept them hovering at three feet, steady despite the sharp gusts that slapped at him, and checked the route.

Up the White River Canyon. Pick up route 410. Climb to the top of the pass along the road.

"Around to Paradise on the south side."

Nearly due west over the lower flanks of Rainier, some good valley and ridge work there.

"And back to base."

Follow the Nisqually River, shoot over Alder Lake and head home.

"One more," Tim suggested with a tone that Henderson was beginning to learn meant trouble. "Hit Box Canyon."

Ouch! Halfway between Cayuse Pass and Paradise, but at the bottom of a deep cleft carved by the Muddy Fork Cowlitz River.

"And your max altitude for this operation," Big John rumbled not to be outdone by his buddy, "is fifty feet…to the top of your rotor."

"C'mon, dude. You got a death wish asking the man to do that?"

And Mark knew at that moment he was committed to it. And the next moment he realized that had been exactly Tim's intent with his complaint. He was definitely going to have to watch out for this pair.

But he had no option to turn away from the challenge or he'd lose face as their commander; totally unacceptable.

Top of rotor below fifty feet meant keeping his wheels below forty. Through canyon switchbacks, winding passes, and unpredictable weather.

He admitted that it was a good challenge; now to make sure it wasn't a lethal one.

"Thirty minutes between each point, Richardson." At full speed, straight flight, he could make each target in under fifteen minutes, but he wanted to nail the height limit as well.

Mark double-checked his fuel, engine temp, and all of the other readings that were his copilot's responsibility. All green and good to go. "I want to hit each arrival plus or minus twenty-five seconds." It wasn't like the big eight-hundred mile Black Route training loops that were a standard part of SOAR training, but it would definitely be a challenge.

"Start the timer…now."

Mark shoved the cyclic forward to tip the nose down for speed and pulled up on the collective just enough to not eat the goal post at the end of the football field, though his wheels passed between the uprights.

"I'd suggest hanging on back there."

7

Michael arrived at the head of Disappointment Cleaver as full dark and the first big slam of the storm arrived together. He'd had to pull his second ice axe to make sure he always had one buried in the snow so that he wasn't blown away.

Charli had missed the one-hour check in and it was a grueling twenty more minutes before he reached her position. And another ten before he found her in the minimal visibility afforded by his headlamp.

She was barely conscious when he arrived and was difficult to rouse from her stupor.

When he did, she hugged him and then she wept. The tears froze on her face and would have sealed her eyes shut if Michael hadn't brushed them clear quickly with his bare fingers.

She'd been telling the truth about being secure. The various lines leading from the ice screw and the piton in the rock face down to her brother all met at her harness. So while she hadn't been under any stress, she'd been solidly pinned against the snow and wholly unable to shift out of the wind or exercise her legs.

She'd kept her arms moving and wore a balaclava, as he did, but her legs had no feeling up past the knees. She needed to get into a hospital fast if she didn't want to be losing toes, feet, or even worse. Her words were already slurring though he couldn't tell if that was hypothermia or altitude sickness.

In minutes he had a Z-harness rigged and was levering Fred Moore back up from the crevasse. He didn't want to think about what he'd find, but it wasn't as if he had a choice.

Except Fred wasn't coming. The rope went taut—and stopped.

Michael rigged a descending harness from the extra lines Charli had draped about her and lowered himself into the crevasse.

The line between the brother and sister had been fifty feet long, about five feet too long for poor Fred. His head had shattered and the blood had frozen to the ice.

Michael sat there for a long moment. In a war zone, you left no man behind. But in a civilian zone like a winter blizzard on Rainier he was less sure? If Michael simply cut the line, the chances of the body being discovered in the next thousand years was minimal until he spilled out in the Muddy Fork Cowlitz River at the base of the creeping glacier. Did Charli, if she lived, really need to see her brother's battered body?

That was assuming that he could keep her alive to get her off the mountain.

Michael kept the dead body company while he dangled close above it and quickly considered the options.

The woman certainly couldn't walk down.

He had a bivy bag that would only fit one person. If Charli and Fred had a tent or sleeping bags, they weren't on their packs. They must still be down at Camp Muir; they'd thought to go light for a fast strike at the summit and a quick return. Pretty standard even if it hadn't worked out this time.

He could rig a sledge, but the dozen or more hours that would require to get her down the mountain safely would be a cruel torture and probably kill any chance for her survival.

Old adage: when all the options suck, come up with a new option.

As gently as he could, he used his axe to chip Fred free of the ice. Then he pulled the parka hood up and over the missing chunk of his skull and snugged the front closure as tight as he could until only a scarf-covered nose showed through. Then he hauled himself back to the surface.

Charli was too far out of it to ask about her brother, so he pulled out his radio.

The park rangers could be of no help here. He did reach them on a patch-through to

Crystal Mountain Ski Resort a couple of peaks to the east. There the signal wasn't blocked by the mass of Disappointment Cleaver.

Michael was relieved that the park rangers had met the older couple most of the way down from Camp Muir and gotten them off the mountain. There was no chance of them setting out again in time to help him.

Well, he might be sitting in what the park rangers clearly thought was a hopeless position. But they lived in a different world than he did.

Michael had long since crossed over into the military world and could see how that completely overlaid the civilian one. It had a network of lines that connected as thoroughly as highways and airlines connected civilians. The American military and its allies formed a complete second layer all over the globe that was mostly invisible—unless you knew how to access it.

Time to try that next layer out.

He switched his radio over to the military radio band.

If that didn't work, he had a satellite radio. It was more typically used for calling in airstrikes, but it would do the job of checking all options if the first one didn't pan out.

He began transmitting on the military emergency frequency.

8

"We've got a Mayday on 243," Richardson spoke up.

Henderson slid to a halt inches above the road in the heart of Cayuse Pass and grinned at the clock. Twenty-four seconds early. He was inside his time window.

Full dark had set in and—Shit!

He yanked up on the collective barely in time to clear a truck that had decided to cross the pass at that moment. He wasn't sure which of them was more surprised.

"Give me audio," he said to cover his nerves.

"Roger, Mayday," Mark kept his voice steady. "This is a Black Hawk out of Fort Lewis-McChord," he certainly wasn't giving his ID to some unknown. "How may we assist?"

"I have a civilian at twelve thousand feet who needs immediate evac to hospital. Plus one."

No need to explain the "Plus one." Plus one corpse.

The guy on the far end of the radio call continued, "Winds currently gusting seven-five to one-one-zero estimated. Temp steady at minus thirty. Visibility under ten feet in driving ice and snow. Can you assist?" The wind howled over his headset while the guy's transmit key was down. No question about mishearing the wind speeds aloft.

The silence on the intercom was deafening after he keyed off. What kind of a crazy bastard was doing a search-and-rescue in those kinds of conditions? The guy was sitting in the middle of a Category 2 hurricane.

Mark considered. He *had* wanted to prove that a DAP Hawk of the 5D could go anywhere and do anything. Hadn't he wished for that just an hour or two ago while standing safely on the tarmac at Fort Lewis?

Twelve thousand feet in the midst of a kick-ass, hurricane-force storm.

What ultimately decided him was one word, "Civilian."

Based on the frequency and the way he spoke, there was a military man on top of that mountain asking for his assistance. And the military's job was to—

"Roger, Mayday. This is—"

Mark released the mike switch. He wasn't sure whether he wanted to announce himself over the radio. "Richardson. Where is this guy? Do you have a vector?" A sharp gust over the pass caused his finger to bump the transmit button and send the last word.

"—vector."

"Roger, Viper. Mayday is at," and he rattled off GPS coordinates that Richardson keyed down for him.

Viper? Mark had said "vector" but over the wind's roar it was miracle they could understand each other at all. Mark also noted that the guy still wasn't identifying himself.

Any normal soldier would do so. Even Green Beret.

Whoever this was had to be extremely well trained to be doing a rescue in this weather and yet wasn't transmitting his identity. That meant only one thing: Special Operations— the standard customers of the Night Stalkers.

And he needed their help.

"Okay guys," Mark called over the intercom. "Dress warm. This elevator is going up." The DAP Hawk was hovering at forty-six hundred feet in Cayuse Pass headed for twelve thou.

"Women's lingerie," Tim started in as they climbed.

"Bowling jerseys, jockstraps, and tap shoes," Big John joined in.

Mark tuned them out as they continued calling out more and more outrageous items.

He considered the best plan of attack as he climbed clear of the trees and ridges and turned west. Staying low had been a rough ride up to Cayuse Pass through all the gusts. Up here the air was smoother, somewhat… and blowing him south like a son of a bitch.

He carved harder to the north in order to aim straight west.

The DAP bucked in a sharp curl of wind and dropped two hundred feet before he could find clear air for the rotors to get a good bite. He added another thousand feet to his altitude, and it got worse.

Low, Mark muttered to himself. It was crazy, but it was what they had just been practicing. Come in low. Close enough to the ground that the worst of the winds were passing above you.

"No rescue basket down to this guy," he called back to the crew chiefs who were off in some strange shopping land of elf hats, reindeer girdles, and replacement runners for your sleigh. "If the wind catches it, it will just brain him. Long line off the winch. If he can catch it, we'll trust to their climbing harnesses. And wrap it in glow sticks. They aren't going to be able to see shit out there."

Tim and John didn't say a word now, which was good because he couldn't afford the distraction as he moved down toward an ice field that he couldn't see, except by radar. It also told him that they didn't need to talk;

he'd given them enough information to figure out the plan without any questions. A huge time saver that he'd have to remember for the future.

He tried the landing lights, but was blinded by the million reflections off the swirling snow. Turbulence or not, he climbed up until his eyes recovered from the momentary blinding enough to again clearly read the radar images on the inside of his visor.

What kind of a lunatic ran a search and rescue operation under these conditions?

9

Michael neither heard nor saw the approaching helicopter. He knew they'd arrived above him when the ice crystals shifted from being driven sideways by the wind from the storm to being driven downward by the wind from the helo's rotors.

A winch line appeared in the middle of the maelstrom whirling about wildly, so he pushed Charli down to lie on the snow and stood over her as he tried to guide them into place over the radio. Fat chance. They couldn't see him, and even if they could, the wind was slapping around the steel cable like a cat with a piece of yarn.

There was no question who was above him. Only a Night Stalker would be out on such a foul night and only a man who completely trusted his own piloting skills would attempt such a rescue.

The first time the glowing green lights tied to the heavy metal hook at the end of the cable came sailing at him, he had to dive down on top of Charli to avoid being clobbered by it. She barely responded with an "oof!" Her time was getting short.

On the next pass the winch hook was moving more slowly and he managed to snag it.

Not trusting that he'd have another success like that, or that he could hold it for long, he immediately spun around and snapped the hook into Charli's harness. He flicked out a knife and severed her ties to the ice screw and piton.

"Lift. Now, now, now!" he called over the radio.

With a surprised squawk, jolted out of her stupor by the sudden yank on her harness, Charli disappeared aloft. Michael stood ready to slash the line connecting her to her brother's body in case it snagged on the side of the crevasse, but moments later Fred's body followed his sister's skyward.

He waited for the report, it didn't take long.

"Civilian aboard." And a few seconds more, "Plus one."

"Roger and thanks."

"Sending winch back down."

"Negative," he was just two thousand feet below the summit and there were two very solid anchors tied to his harness. "Negative. I'm good here. Thanks, Mayday out."

Whoever was flying the helicopter was silent for a long moment, swore succinctly on air, and then was gone.

Michael called the Park Rangers to let them know it was okay to stand down. Then he dug a shelf into the snow, pulled out his bivy bag, and slid in to ride out the peace within the heart of the storm.

10

Michael came down off the mountain three days later. The storm had blown hard for two days and then he'd taken the summit beneath a sunny sky on a dead calm day. The temperature steady around minus sixty, he had owned the peak and his extra days at altitude had given him the acclimation to spend some time enjoying the vistas in every direction from the wide crater's rim that capped the old volcano.

He still didn't have any better answers to his career.

If he left The Unit…

There simply wasn't anything challenging enough on the other side of that coin. He was never one of those serve-a-couple-tours-and-get-out kind of guys. He was a lifer, but what was the next step from Delta?

CIA's Special Activities Division had tried to recruit him a couple times. While he enjoyed the black ops, the S.A.D. was just a little too much wash-your-hands-after-even-talking-to-them kind of guys.

The Activity, the slickest field intel guys that the nation's military had ever come up with, was tempting. But it wasn't the kind of challenge he liked. He enjoyed being at the tip of the spear.

After he dug his truck out of a couple feet of snow, he drove down from Paradise on the plowed out road and signed out at the Ranger Station in Longmire. Apparently news of his rescue was the big talk of park's ranger staff. They were sorely disappointed when he refused to meet with any media. A Delta operator's photo smack on the front page of the Tacoma News Tribune would not play well back at Fort Bragg. He should never have used his real name in the register.

He escaped as quickly as he could and went into the National Park Inn for a meal. It was one of those Depression-era lodges built by the government on a grand scale to put the nation back to work. Log-built, generous veranda, high, gabled roof. It was equally grand inside, the massive lobby had enough room to play a fair game of hockey except for the deep couches. High ceilings held up by massive log rafters. He headed for the restaurant seating down at the far end of the massive space.

Michael ordered the turkey blue plate special, heavy on the gravy, and the roast beef platter as well. He'd burned a lot of calories over the last four days. He'd managed to squeeze in a summiting of Little Tahoma Peak on the way down just for completeness sake. The Congo Rainforest still lay two days away.

He chose a seat with his back to the wall. As always.

Exit to the kitchen was to his left. At the other end of the wide lobby was the entrance to the lodge. Big, timber-built doors led in from the outside partway along the right-hand wall. The cathedral ceiling was filled with the light reflected off the heavy layers of snow outside the long bank of front windows. A grandfather clock, stately in a heavy Doug Fir cabinet, chimed the hour.

He was done with the turkey and half-way through the roast beef when a man walked in through the double doors. Many people had come in and out while Michael was eating, fourteen women and nine men in seven separate groups. Each one with the earmarks of a tourist: chattering, expensive if not the most sensible snow gear, cameras.

This man was tall, broad-shouldered, and alone. He wore an expensive leather bomber jacket that said tourist and worn jeans and heavy boots that didn't. He wore mirrored Ray Bans and stood in the center of the main room doing a slow turn as he assessed the lobby and restaurant seating and everyone in it. His stance said "trained soldier" as did his careful inspection. His body silence said Special Operations.

His eyes passed over Michael…and then swung back.

The pilot.

He strode across the room, covertly continuing his assessment of people and exits, though not in any way that would be noticed except by another trained soldier. Without asking he sat down across from Michael with his back to the lobby, something Michael would never do.

Then the man took off his mirrored sunglasses and set them on the table without folding in the earpieces, so that the lens were only slightly tilted. He looked down and gave the glasses a slight nudge.

Michael judged angles and decided that the man had chosen well. Anything he couldn't see directly, he could keep an eye on in the mirrors of the sunglasses, which reflected the goings-on behind him. He'd have to remember that trick.

"The girl's okay," the pilot began speaking without introduction. "Lost a couple of toes and a brother. But she's fine."

Michael nodded. Good news.

"Really wants to thank you."

Michael shook his head, not gonna happen.

"She's a real looker under all that snow gear. Blond, tall, very athletic body."

Clearly this man's type. Still, not gonna happen. Michael wasn't sure if he had a type, but Nightingale-effect gratitude wasn't something he was after.

The pilot ordered the roast beef when a waitress came around. Michael ordered a slice of blueberry pie with ice cream.

They sat in comfortable silence until they were served.

"I know a guy who talks as little as you," the man who still hadn't introduced himself cut into his beef and sighed with pleasure. "Not Montana roast like my parents' beef, but not too shabby."

Michael had never had Montana beef. Especially not ranch fresh.

"My dad was a SEAL for almost twenty years. Doesn't speak unless he has something to say."

SEAL dad. Night Stalker son.

"Dad never was a big fan of ice and snow; shoveled it for too many Montana winters is his excuse. I expect it was because it froze up the fishing streams for too many months each year. He and I spent a lot of good time standing in those streams."

Michael would agree. Ice and snow he could take or leave. But he loved the quiet times of fishing.

"Strikes me that camping on that mountain top in the middle of a storm with an attitude was more the style of an operator from The Unit than a SEAL. Damned nice piece of work, by the way. Got some of the details out of the park rangers. Though your name led nowhere—I was able to verify you exist, but otherwise an absolute dead end—another sure Delta sign. Got some more of the details from the grateful babe. Very grateful. Sure you're not interested?"

Michael was sure; he was headed back to the Congo in thirty-six hours and had never been a big fan of a casual screw. He ate some of the blueberry pie which was exceptional. The wild blueberries were probably picked right out here on the mountain slopes last summer and frozen.

So, the man was smart enough to figure out that he was with the Special Forces

Operational Detachment-Delta, which Michael would never confirm nor deny.

"I'm putting together a new company," the pilot's tone became more businesslike, more intense. This man cared deeply about the next part of the conversation.

He didn't need to identify SOAR, he'd know that Michael had figured that much out on his own. Michael appreciated that the man didn't waste time on useless words.

"I'm getting the very best people. I've stolen the Number One mechanic and gunner out of 1st Battalion, pissed their commanders off pretty good. Found a co-pilot out of the 3rd. I've snared the Number One teams in Chinook and Little Birds too. I'm building a blended Company, not just all one platform."

"Flexibility," Michael spoke for the first time. The military was not the most flexible structure; it was something The Unit prided themselves on but few others could get away with or even wrap their heads around at a true operational level.

"Precisely!" the pilot leaned forward eagerly. "I want a company that can dynamically adapt to any situation. I want you."

Michael stopped with his fork halfway up in the air, "Me?"

The man nodded and returned his attention to his roast beef. A couple came in, their designer clothes covered with the tell-tale patches of a snowball fight. The pilot's eyes flicked down to inspect the reflection in his glasses and he smiled for a moment before returning his attention to his meal.

"Doing what?"

The man shrugged, "We'll figure that out as we go. An embedded Delta liaison? A permanently-attached squad for fast reaction, trained to maximize leverage of the DAP heli-platform? How the hell should I know. I'm after the right people first. Then the team will drive itself to excel as it comes together."

A DAP. He hadn't dropped that casually; it was a symbol of just how much the military was impressed by this man. The rescue helicopter had been a DAP—in the heart of a blizzard atop the most lethal mountain in the lower forty-eight states. This guy wasn't just blowing smoke; he was out on the cutting edge.

It would be a hell of a challenge.

Michael would miss The Unit...but then he wouldn't really be leaving, would he?

And a team that could develop synergistic-ally from the interactions of a half dozen different disciplines?

New information and challenges from the very best pilots on the planet to the very best technological innovations. And a commander who wasn't all hoo-rah but rather understood the silence of fishing, of being out in nature.

He finished his blueberry pie as the pilot polished off his roast beef.

Michael kept inspecting the possibilities as he would any pending operation, but could find no tactical or strategic hole in the plan. If the man was as good as his word, which he'd proved by doing that rescue, then it should work. In fact, it could set up a whole new model for inter-operability, always a fascinating problem.

Michael decided he wasn't just in, he was in all the way.

"What's your name?"

The man pushed aside his empty plate, kicked back and rested his feet on another chair. He pulled on his mirrored shades as if saying he completely trusted Michael to have his back.

He grinned like he'd just won the best poker hand on the planet.

"Viper. Viper Henderson."

Then they both started to laugh.

About the Author

M. L. Buchman has over 30 novels in print. His military romantic suspense books have been named Barnes & Noble and NPR "Top 5 of the year" and Booklist "Top 10 of the Year." In addition to romance, he also writes thrillers, fantasy, and science fiction.

In among his career as a corporate project manager he has: rebuilt and single-handed a fifty-foot sailboat, both flown and jumped out of airplanes, designed and built two houses, and bicycled solo around the world. He is now making his living as a full-time writer on the Oregon Coast with his beloved wife. He is constantly amazed at what you can do with a degree in Geophysics. You may keep up with his writing by subscribing to his newsletter at

www.mlbuchman.com.

Bring On the Dusk!
-Michael's story-

There were few times that Colonel Michael Gibson of Delta Force appreciated the near-psychotic level of commitment displayed by terrorists, but this was one of those times. If they hadn't been so rigid in even their attire, his disguise would have been much more difficult.

The al-Qaeda terrorist training camp deep in the Yemeni desert required that all of their hundred new trainees dress in white with black headdresses that left only the eyes exposed. The thirty-four trainers were dressed similarly but wholly in black, making them easy to distinguish. They were also the only ones armed, which was a definite advantage.

The camp's dress code made for a perfect cover. The four men of his team wore loose-fitting black robes like the trainers. Lieutenant Bill Bruce used dark contacts to hide his blue eyes and they all had rubbed a dye onto their hands and wrists, the only other uncovered portion of their bodies.

Michael and his team had parachuted into the deep desert the night before and traveled a quick ten kilometers on foot before burying themselves in the sand along the edges of the main training grounds. Only their faces were exposed, each carefully hidden by a thorn bush.

The midday temperatures had easily blown through a hundred and ten degrees. It felt twice that inside the heavy clothing and lying under a foot of hot sand, but uncomfortable was a way of life in "The Unit," as Delta Force called itself, so this was of little concern. They'd dug deep enough so that they weren't simply roasted alive, even if it felt that way by the end of the motionless day.

It was three minutes to sunset, three minutes until the start of Maghrib, the fourth scheduled prayer of the five that were performed daily.

At the instant of sunset, the muezzin began chanting *adhan*, the call to prayer.

Thinking themselves secure in the deep desert of the Abyan province of southern Yemen, every one of the trainees and the trainers knelt and faced northwest toward Mecca.

After fourteen motionless hours— fewer than a dozen steps from a hundred and thirty terrorists—moving smoothly and naturally was a challenge as Michael rose from his hiding place. He shook off the sand and swung his AK-47 into a comfortable position. The four of them approached the prostrate group in staggered formation from the southeast over a small hillock.

The Delta operators interspersed themselves among the other trainers and knelt, blending in perfectly. Of necessity, they all spoke enough Arabic to pass if questioned.

Michael didn't check the others because that might draw attention. If they hadn't made it cleanly into place, an alarm would have been raised and the plan would have changed drastically. All was quiet, so he listened to the muezzin's words and allowed himself to settle into the peace of the prayer.

Bismi-llāhi r-rahmāni r-rahīm…

In the name of Allah, the most compassionate, the most merciful…

He sank into the rhythm and meaning of it—not as these terrorists twisted it in the name of murder and warfare, but as it was actually stated. Moments like this one drove home the irony of his long career to become the most senior field operative in Delta while finding an inner quiet in the moment before dealing death.

Perhaps in their religious fervor, the terrorists found the same experience. But what they lacked was flexibility. They wound themselves up to throw away their lives, if necessary, to complete their preprogrammed actions exactly as planned.

For Michael, an essential centering in self allowed perfect adaptability when situations went kinetic—Delta's word for the shit unexpectedly hitting the fan.

That was Delta's absolute specialty.

Starting with zero preconceptions in either energy or strategy allowed for the perfect action that fit each moment in a rapidly changing scenario. Among the team, they'd joke sometimes about how Zen, if not so Buddhist, the moment before battle was.

And, as always, he accepted the irony of that with no more than a brief smile at life's whimsy.

Dealing death was one significant part of what The Unit did.

U.S. SFOD-D, Special Forces Operational Detachment-Delta, went where no other fighting force could go and did what no one else could do.

Today, it was a Yemeni terrorist training camp.

Tomorrow would take care of itself.

They were the U.S. Army's Tier One asset and no one, except their targets, would ever know they'd been here. One thing for certain, had The Unit been unleashed on bin Laden, not a soul outside the command structure would know who'd been there. SEAL Team Six had done a top-notch job, but talking about it wasn't something a Delta operator did. But Joint Special Operations Command's leader at the time was a former STS member, so the SEALs had gone in instead.

Three more minutes of prayer.

Then seven minutes to help move the trainees into their quarters where they would be locked in under guard for the night, as they were still the unknowns.

Or so the trainers thought.

Three more minutes to move across the compound through the abrupt fall of darkness in the equatorial desert to where the commanders would meet for their evening meal and evaluation of the trainees.

After that the night would get interesting.

Bismi-llāhi r-rahmāni r-rahīm...

In the name of Allah, the most compassionate, the most merciful...

***

Captain Claudia Jean Casperson of the U.S. Army's 160th Special Operations Aviation Regiment—commonly known as the Night Stalkers—finally arrived at the aircraft carrier in the Gulf of Aden after two full days in transit from Fort Campbell, Kentucky.

The Gulf of Aden ran a hundred miles wide and five hundred long between Somalia in Africa and Yemen on the southern edge of the Arabian Peninsula. The Gulf connected the Suez Canal and the Red Sea at one end to the Indian Ocean on the other, making it perhaps the single busiest and most hazardous stretch of water on the planet.

Claudia tried to straighten her spine after she climbed off the C-2 Greyhound twin-engine cargo plane. It was the workhorse of carrier onboard delivery and, from the passenger's point of view, the loudest plane ever designed. If not, it certainly felt that way. Shaking her head didn't clear the buzz of the twin Allison T56 engines from either her ears or the

pounding of the two big eight-bladed pro-
pellers from her body.

A deckhand clad in green, which identified
him as a helicopter specialist, met her before
she was three steps off the rear ramp. He
took her duffel without a word and started
walking away, the Navy's way of saying,
"Follow me." She resettled her rucksack
across her shoulders and followed like a
one-woman jet fighter taxiing along after
her own personal ground guidance truck.

Rather than leading her to quarters, the
deckhand took her straight to an MH-6M
Little Bird helicopter perched on the edge
of the carrier's vast deck. That absolutely
worked for her. As soon as they had her
gear stowed in the tiny back compartment,
he turned to her and handed her a slip of
paper.

"This is the current location, contact
frequency, and today's code word for landing
authorization for your ship. They need this
bird returned today and you just arrived,
so that works out. It's fully fueled. They're
expecting you." He rattled off the tower
frequency for the carrier's air traffic con-

trol tower, saluted, and left her to prep her aircraft before she could salute back.

Thanks for the warm welcome to the theater of operations.

This wasn't a war zone. But it wasn't far from one either, she reminded herself. Would saying, "Hi," have killed him? That almost evoked a laugh; she hadn't exactly been chatty herself. Word count for the day so far, one, saying thanks to the C-2 crewman who'd rousted her from a bare doze just thirty seconds before landing.

The first thing she did was get into her full kit. She pulled her flight suit on over her clothes, tucking her long blond hair down her back inside the suit. Full armor brought the suit to about thirty pounds. She shrugged on a Dragon Skin vest that she'd purchased herself to give double protection over her torso. Over that, her SARVSO survival vest and finally her FN-SCAR rifle across her chest and her helmet on her head. Total gear about fifty pounds. As familiar as a second skin; she always felt a little exposed without it.

Babe in armor.

Who would have thought a girl from nowhere Arizona would be standing on an aircraft carrier off the Arabian Peninsula in full fighter gear?

If anyone were to ask, she'd tell them it totally rocked. Actually, she'd shrug and acknowledge that she was proud to be here… but she'd be busy thinking that it totally rocked.

The Little Bird was the smallest helicopter in any division of the U.S. military, and that made most people underestimate it. Not Claudia, she loved the Little Bird. It was a tough and sassy craft with a surprising amount of power for its small size. The helo also operated far more independently than any other aircraft in the inventory and, to Claudia's way of thinking, that made the Little Bird near perfect.

The tiny chopper seated two up front and didn't have any doors, so the wide opening offered the pilot an excellent field of view. The fact that it also offered the enemy a wide field of fire is why Claudia wore the secondary Dragon Skin vest. The helicopter could seat two in back, if they were desperate—the space was small enough that Claudia's ruck and duffel filled much of it. On the attack version, the rear space would be filled with cans of ammunition.

In Special Operations Forces, the action teams rode on the outside of Little Birds. This one was rigged with a bench seat along either side that could fold down to transport three combat soldiers on either side.

Claudia wanted an attack bird, not a transport, but she'd fight that fight once she reached her assigned company. For now she was simply glad to be a pilot who'd been deemed "mission ready" for the 160th SOAR.

She went through the preflight, found the bird as clean as every other Night Stalker craft, and powered up for the flight. Less than a hundred miles, so she'd be there in forty minutes. Maybe then she could sleep.

***

As the rapid onset of full dark in the desert swept over the Yemeni desert, Michael and Bill moved up behind the main building that was used by the terrorist camp's training staff. It was a one-story, six-room structure. Concrete slab, cinder-block walls, metal roof. Doors front and back. The heavy-metal rear one was locked, but they had no intention of using it anyway.

The intel from the MQ-1C Gray Eagle drone that the Night Stalkers' intel staff had kept circling twenty thousand feet overhead for the last three nights had indicated that four command-level personnel met here each night. Most likely position was in the southeast corner room. Four of the other rooms were barrack spaces that wouldn't be used until after the trainers had all eaten together at the chow tent. The sixth room was the armory.

Dry bread and water had been the fare for the trainees. Over the next few months they would be desensitized to physical dis-comfort much as a Delta operator was. Too little food, too little sleep, and too much exercise, especially early on, to weed out the weak or uncommitted.

He and Bill squatted beneath the southeast window that faced away from the center of the camp; only the vast, dark desert lay beyond. Shifting the AK-47s over their shoulders, they unslung their preferred weapons—Heckler & Koch HK416 carbine rifles with flash suppressors that made them nearly silent.

Bill pulled out a small fiber-optic camera and slipped it up over the windowsill. As they squatted out of sight, the small screen gave them a view of the inside of the target building for the first time.

Not four men but eight were seated on cushions around a low table bearing a large teapot. Michael recognized five from various briefings, three of them Tier One targets. They'd only been expecting one Tier One.

A long table sported a half-dozen laptops, and a pair of file cabinets stood at one end. They hadn't counted on that at all. This was supposed to be a training camp, not an operations center.

They were going to need more help to take advantage of the new situation.

Michael got on the radio.

***

"USS Peleliu. This is Captain Casperson in Little Bird…" She didn't know the name of the bird. She read off the tail number from the small plate on the control panel. "Inbound from eighty miles at two-niner-zero."

You didn't want to sneak up on a ship of war that could shoot you down at this distance if they were in a grouchy mood.

"Roger that, Captain. Status?"

"Flying solo, full fuel."

"In your armor?"

"Roger that." Why in the world would they… Training. They'd want to make sure she wasn't ignoring her training. Kid stuff. She'd flown Cobra attack birds for the U.S. Marines for six years before her transfer and spent two more years training with the Night Stalkers. She wasn't an—

"This is Air Mission Commander Archie Stevens." A different voice came on the air. "Turn immediate heading three-four-zero. Altitude five-zero feet, all speed. You'll be joining a flight ten miles ahead of you for an exfil. We can't afford to slow them down until you make contact, so hustle."

She slammed over the cyclic control in her right hand to shift to the new heading.

Okay, maybe not so much a training test.

Exfil. Exfiltration. A ground team needed to be pulled out and pulled out now. She'd done it in a hundred drills, so she kept calm and hoped that her voice sounded that way. She expected that it didn't.

"Uh, Roger." Claudia had dozed fitfully for six hours in the last three days, and most of that had been in a vibrator seat on the roaring C-2 Greyhound. No rest for the weary.

Once on the right heading, she dove into the night heading for fifty feet above the ocean waves and opened up the throttles to the edge of the never-exceed speed of a hundred and seventy-five miles per hour.

The adrenaline had her wide awake before she reached her flight level.

***

Available at fine retailers everywhere

More information at:
www.mlbuchman.com

Made in the USA
Columbia, SC
28 January 2018